How to Act Like a Responsible, Almost-Adult

Dave and Neta Jackson

Story and characters based on the
Mini-Movie™ of the same name
Story by George Taweel & Rob Loos,
Teleplay by Martha Williamson

Nashville, Tennessee

BROADMAN & HOLMAN PUBLISHERS

TAWEEL-LOOS & COMPANY
"The mini-movie™ Studio"

"SNAP" is based on the characters created by
George Taweel & Rob Loos. Story by George Taweel & Rob Loos.
Teleplay written by Martha Williamson. © 1993.

4240-05
0-8054-4005-4

Dewey Decimal Classification: JF
Subject Heading: HUMAN RELATIONS - FICTION
Library of Congress Card Catalog Number: 94-609
Printed in the United States of America

Library of Congress Cataloging-in-Publication Data

Jackson, Dave.
Snap : how to act like a responsible almost-adult / by Dave and Neta Jackson.
"Based on the video of the same name created by George Taweel & Rob Loos."
p. cm. — (Secret adventures ; #2)
Summary: Thirteen-year-old Drea learns a lesson about responsibility when she's forced to cancel her exciting weekend plans to baby-sit for Rebecca and Matt.
ISBN 0-8054-4005-4
[1. Responsibility—Fiction. 2. Baby-sitters—Fiction. 3. Christian life—Fiction.] I. Jackson, Neta. II. Taweel, George. III. Loos, Rob. IV. Title. V. Series: Jackson, Dave. Secret adventures; #2.
PZ7.J132418Si 1994
[Fic]—dc20 94-609
CIP

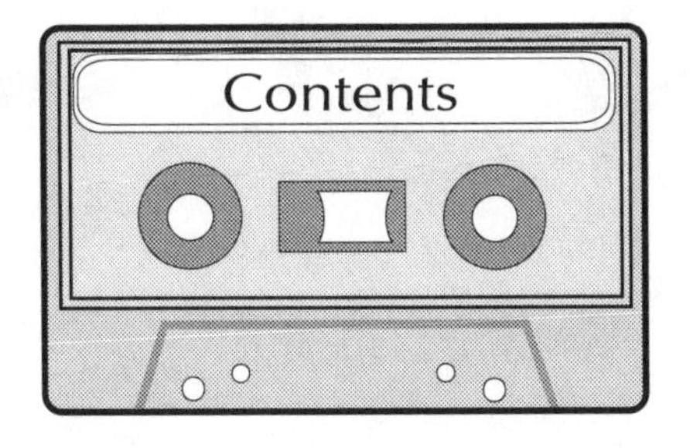
Contents

From everyone who has been given much, much will be demanded; and from the one who has been entrusted with much, much more will be asked.

—Luke 12:48b, NIV

The Amazing Shrinking Vest

It's Day 4,854 in the Secret Adventures of Drea Thomas. Time: ten hundred hours—that's ten a.m. for ordinary civilians—and . . . pardon the background noise, E.D. It's only my gym shoes in the dryer. That's one problem using this Walkman as an *electronic diary*—I pick up all these signals from "outer space." Hmmm . . . guess in the case of the clothes dryer, it's picking up noise from "inner space."

But frankly, E.D., having to do my own laundry on a gorgeous fall Saturday is not what I'd call an "amazing adventure." In fact, I wonder if it qualifies as cruel and unusual punishment to a minor?

Hmm . . . I better check on those shoes in the dryer . . . I'll just open the door and take a peek . . .

Suddenly the gym shoes come flying out of the clothes dryer, followed by my jeans, vests, and T-shirts whizzing past me in a blur. As I watch in amazement, the shoes land with a thump on the kitchen table, morphing before my eyes into a black-robed judge with triple chins. A motley assortment of my clothes lines up to one side, jostling for position as a panel of jurors . . . except for one pair of jeans and a T-shirt, which stand apart, morphing in a blink into the figure of an attractive woman who looks vaguely familiar.

Mom!

The judge with the triple chins glowers over the edge of the kitchen table—no, it's now a great oak desk!—at the quaking woman standing before him.

"Mrs. Laurie Thomas, are you the mother of the plaintiff, Drea Thomas?"

My thirtysomething mother nods. "I . . . I am, Your Honor."

"And are you pleading GUILTY to the charge of making your thirteen-year-old daughter do her own laundry?"

I see Mom look down at the toes of her shoes. "Yes," she whispers. "It's true."

The chins quiver with astonishment at such blatant disregard for child labor laws. "Then I sentence you to forty more years as marketing

director for Jamison's Department Store . . . and NO GOLD WATCH upon retirement!"

"Oh, no . . . " gasps my distraught mother. "Not forty more years . . .!"

Then, in a zip, judge, jury, and plaintiff dissolve into a whirling mass of shoes, jeans, T-shirts, and vests which spin like a miniature tornado into the clothes dryer, closing the door behind them with a—

Bang!

The noise of the clothes dryer door banging shut brings me back to reality in a SNAP. Wow . . . my imagination is working overtime today.

But . . . I don't think "cruel and unusual punishment" would hold up in court after all. *Sigh.* Doing laundry is just another one of Mom's Great Ideas—that I'm old enough to take responsibility for my own clothes. I'm sure the idea sounds good to parent-types in theory . . . but figure it this way, E.D.

There's only three of us in our family, right? Well, four, if you count Grandpa, but he doesn't actually live here or do his laundry at our house. . . . Anyway, there's just Dad, Mom, and me, and when Mom does the laundry, our clothes make nice, decent-size loads of, ya know, whites, wash-and-wear, darks, and . . . whatever—ya know, the stuff you're supposed to wash in COLD water. But today, when I tried to sort my clothes into all those categories like Mom suggested—all I got was dinky little piles, not enough for any one to make a load!

Now, E.D., don't you agree it'd be more energy efficient and cost effective to do the laundry cooperatively? Large loads, less time, less electricity . . .

Hmm. Gotta be careful here. If I push this point, Mom might suggest that I do the laundry for the whole family! Oh, well . . . I combined all those dinky loads into just "lights" and "darks" anyway—can't make that big a difference, can it? Just because I've become a laundry drudge doesn't mean I can't think up shortcuts!—

Oh, hi, Grandpa! Didn't hear you come in . . . No, Mom and Dad aren't here—they went to the hardware store to pick out wallpaper for the dining room. . . . Do I remember that I promised to help you weed the garden today? Why, uh . . . uh, sure! That's why I'm sitting here on top of the clothes dryer, just waitin' for ya!—

Riiiiiiinng.

—Oh, gotta get the phone. You go on out, Grandpa—I'll be there in a minute . . . or three.

Sigh. Cinderella signing off, E.D.

— Click! —

Sorry I'm back again so soon, E.D., but . . . guess who that was on the phone? Mrs. Long, my principal at Hampton Falls Junior High! She wants me to baby-sit her kids, Rebecca and Matt, for a whole weekend here at my house while she goes to a principals' conference! . . . Oh, yeah, and she wants to know if their English sheepdog, Floyd, can come along. Guess he freaks if they leave him at the kennel. Good ol' Floyd . . . he's the one that looks like an overgrown dust mop.

I hate giving up a whole weekend to baby-sit, but it could be kinda fun—and the extra money will be great! I need to ask Mom and Dad if it's okay for the kids to come here . . . but when did Mrs. Long say she needed me? Umm, I *think* she said weekend after next—guess I better write that down—

Blaaaaaaaaaaaaaat.

—Yikes! Whazzat? Ohhh, yes, the dryer buzzer.

Oh, no! Wha'appened to my new vest? It—it shrank! And I bought it to wear to Cristan Canter's birthday bash next weekend! Wait . . . isn't there some little tag or something—here it is . . .

"Hand wash only, lay flat to dry."

Oh, great. Real bright, Drea Thomas.

— *Click!* —

Checkin' in, E.D. It's now after dinner on Day 4,854 . . . Just finished folding my laundry. All those piles of clean clothes do make me feel kinda good—all except for a certain "micro" vest. Looks like it would fit a Smurf after its trip through the clothes dryer . . . and I definitely feel "blue" about it.

Okay, so I wasn't in the best mood when I went out to help Grandpa this morning. Ever since he retired from the railroad, he's been on a crusade about our poor neglected vegetable garden. Anyway . . . he gave me a pair of garden gloves and pointed to the weeds. But it seemed the more weeds I pulled, the more they multiplied. And it got outrageously hot, too, working in the sunshine—you'd think it was summer instead of a fall weekend.

Finally I threw in the trowel. "Nothing personal, Grandpa," I said, "but I'm sick of weeding."

Didn't faze Grandpa. "Okay," he shrugged, "then I'll pull weeds for a while and you can pick up snails." And he tried to hand me the bucket he'd been filling with garden snails.

"Ewww . . . no thanks," I said.

Suddenly weeding didn't look half bad. I mean, snails in fish tanks are one thing. But picking up those yukky garden critters is another. Even

Cinderella has her limits!

"Hey, if we could train the snails to pull out the weeds, then we wouldn't have to worry about the garden at all," I said, jerking out another clump of weeds, roots and all.

Grandpa laughed and turned his baseball cap backwards, so he looked like the dudes at school—well, except for the suspenders. "Nice try, Drea," he said, "but the snails aren't responsible for this garden . . . we are."

There was that word again: *responsible*. Ugh!

"Grandpa," I complained, "it seems like the older I get, the more responsibilities I'm stuck with—keeping my room clean, doing piles of homework, baby-sitting, even doing my own laundry. . . ."

Grandpa sat back on his heels and nodded, like he understood. "Look at it this way, Drea . . . you only get responsibility when someone trusts you." Then he quoted something . . . I think he said it was from the Gospel of Luke: "From everyone who has been given much, much will be demanded, and from the one who has been entrusted with much, much more will be asked."

I told him it sounded suspiciously like a sermon by Great-grandpa Thomas to me. Ya see, E.D., Grandpa's father was a preacher, and he had a Bible saying ready for every occasion. What's more amazing, is that Grandpa remembers so many of them!

Grandpa grinned. "Yep . . . my father used to tell

us that caring for a garden was good training for life. Ya can't just weed every now and then . . . it takes a whole season of responsibility to make a garden grow."

Or learn how NOT to shrink one's favorite vest in the clothes dryer, I thought.

I looked at the vines dripping with late season tomatoes. They sure looked fat and juicy. I know they didn't get that way with a "snap" of the fingers. Grandpa worked hard all spring and summer.

"So," I said, blinking my baby browns innocently, "if I'm responsible for these tomatoes, maybe someday I can move up to asparagus?"

Grandpa was quick on the draw. "Yep," he shot back at me, "that's the *spear*-it . . . get it?"

"Very *corn*-y, Grandpa," I said, rolling my eyes.

Grandpa stood up and picked up the bucket of snails. "Uh . . . we better *leaf*, before these puns get any worse."

I couldn't let him have the last pun.

"That's a *berry* responsible idea, Grandpa," I said, jumping up and following him into the house for a cold drink. He just put his arm around me and laughed. Which is what I like about Grandpa, E.D. . . . he really listens to me when I have a problem, and takes me seriously . . . but not so seriously that we can't have a good laugh about it.

Oh! Speaking of being responsible, I better go ask Mom and Dad right now whether the Long kids can stay here for a whole weekend in . . . what was it again? A couple weeks, I think . . . yeah, pretty sure.

So, E.D., as Grandpa would say, *lettuce* sign off for now.

— *Click!* —

P.S. before bed . . .

I got the green light for baby-sitting the Long kids, E.D. Mom said she and Dad ought to be done with the assault on the dining room by then . . . they're hoping to get it redecorated next weekend. Right now they're downstairs . . . uh, politely arguing . . . about whether to wallpaper or paint, and whether the dining room should be muted and Victorian or bold and modern.

Guess I'll stay out of it. At least they let me decorate my attic bedroom the way I want.

That's the good news. The bad news is that I've ruined my best vest, which means I don't have anything new to wear to Cristan Canter's birthday party next Friday night, unless I go shopping . . . but once I buy Cristan's birthday present, I won't have any more money till I get paid for my marathon baby-sitting stint—which isn't for two weeks.

Wait a minute, E.D. . . . why is my dirty sock "walking" across the floor? . . . Uh! What's this lump inside . . . Eewww! a stupid snail! *Grandpa!*

— *Click!* —

The Great Mind Blank

It's only Monday night, E.D. . . . uh, make that the evening of Day 4,856 . . . and already I need another weekend! Groan. All the teachers at Hampton Falls Junior High must have gotten together and come up with a brilliant plan: "How to Pile on More Homework Than Drea Thomas Has Seen in Her Whole Life." On top of all the regular stuff, I've got an English essay due Friday . . . plus an art project . . . not to mention a math test on integers!

Don't they know I have to baby-sit the Long kids three afternoons this week—PLUS squeeze in a shopping trip to buy a gift for Cristan Canter's birthday party on Friday?

Which reminds me. Cristan came up to me in

the cafeteria today, looking like she'd just eaten brussels sprouts. "Oh, Drea," she wailed, "I desperately need your help! My mom told me *I* have to plan some kind of activity for my birthday party Friday night . . . but I can't think of a thing!"

This was news. Cristan Canter's birthday parties are legendary. In first grade her parents gave pony rides on a Shetland pony . . . then there was the clown . . . followed by a magician . . . and somewhere in there was the disastrous birthday bash at Party Palace when Arlene Blake broke her ankle bouncing out of the "moon walk." At least last year they began treating us like teenagers and let her have a sleepover—with fifteen girls from the sixth grade. I'm not sure whose idea it was to dye each other's hair at two in the morning . . . but I don't think Raven Black ever came out of her mother's towels.

So Cristan's parties have something of a reputation to live up to. But I must have scrambled my brains in a Salad Shooter, because I heard myself saying, "Not to worry, Cristan! You order the pizzas, and I'll think of something to razzle-dazzle the guests. Deal?"

She looked so relieved I probably could have asked her to clean my room for a year, and she would've said yes.

As it is, I'm stuck cleaning my own room for the rest of my life, which is probably what I deserve . . .

because I can't think of *anything*. Zip. Zero. I baby-sat Rebecca and Matt Long after school today, and they tried to help. But Rebecca's idea of a really cool blast was a Scrabble tournament . . . and Matt's was touch football.

"Thanks, guys," I told 'em, "but I don't think so."

What am I gonna do, E.D.? Now I'm stuck with a responsibility I'm not sure I want. If I don't think of something soon, Hampton Falls, New Jersey, may be dropped from the Who's Who Birthday Bash Book . . . just kidding. But I gotta do better than Scrabble and touch football, or my name will be MUD, and I'll never be able to show my face at school again.

Groan. Maybe I'll ask my parents—see if they have any ideas . . .

— Click! —

Well, E.D., I'm back. That was about as productive as Christmas tree shopping in July. My parents had paint on the brain . . . when I asked for party ideas, my dad said, "Sure. Bring all your friends over here and we'll put 'em to work painting the dining room. That way we could get it done in, say, twenty minutes . . ."

Yeah, right.

As long as I was downstairs, I decided that a pre-homework snack of cinnamon toast and hot chocolate might help "the little gray cells" in my brain start perking. So I went into the kitchen and dropped two pieces of raisin bread into our antique toaster's slots . . .

"Hey! What's this?" said the toaster, shaking himself as if waking from a snooze. "Ain't it a little late to be making toast? Or maybe you forgot: I don't 'do' evenings."

I looked at the toaster, whose gleaming chrome sides and rounded top made a perfect mirror . . . which was always morphing into a comical face with big eyes, a huge Jimmy Durante nose, and speaking to me in a gravelly voice.

"Hi, Mr. Toaster," I said, with a firm push on the toaster's 'Down' handle. "Sorry to make you work nights, ol' buddy, but I've got a long evening ahead of me. You should see the leaning tower of homework waiting for me up in my room—"

"That ain't nothin'," the Toaster interrupted. "Why, when I was just a tin fork holding a slice of sourdough bread over a campfire . . ."

"Ah-ha! So that's why you're always burning my toast on one side!" I complained, popping up the handle and snatching the raisin bread out onto a plate. "But maybe you can help me anyway," I said, buttering the toast and covering

it with cinnamon sugar. "My friend Cristan put me in charge of entertainment at her birthday party. Got any bright ideas?"

The toaster, who had been pouting, perked up. "No prob-lem-o. Just take me along, plug me in, and ask the party-goers to stick metal forks into my slots. We'll give them an electrifying time they'll never forget!" To prove his point, the toaster sent a jolt of electricity sizzling from one slot to the other . . . and ended up dangling by his cord over the side of the counter.

"Help! Help!" yelled the toaster. "Toaster overboard! Haul me up, matey! Beam me up, Scottie! Please don't leave me hangin', marshal . . ."

I rescued the toaster and waggled a finger at him. "Serves you right. You're the one always lecturing me about NEVER sticking anything metal into the slots of a toaster . . ."

I decided my imagination was getting out of hand, E.D. Mr. Toaster's dumb idea was making "touch football" sound pretty good by comparison!

Oh, well. I better get started on that English composition. I'm seriously considering a new topic for my personal essay: "Fifteen Reasons Why I Will Never Volunteer for Anything Ever Again."

Groan. Five days till party time and counting . . .

— *Click!* —

Countdown: Wednesday night—otherwise known as Day 4,858 in the Secret Adventures of Drea Thomas—and it's already twenty-one hundred hours.

Only three days to go, E.D., and my mind is still in neutral! I finally called Cristan tonight to tell her I don't have any ideas for her party . . . but before I could confess, she said, "Oh, Drea, I'm so glad you're in charge of the entertainment. This is the first time I've ever had boys at my birthday party, and I want it to be a real blast. You're a lifesaver!"

She rattled on about how much she was counting on me, but my mind was stuck on one word: *boys.*

Uh, like, I didn't know there were going to be boys at Cristan Canter's birthday party, E.D. . . . Not that I mind! But it does raise one or two eensy-teensy problems.

One: Mom and Dad have already said yes to Cristan's party . . . but they're assuming it's an all-girl thing, because it always has been before. What if they change their minds? I mean, you never can tell how parents are gonna react when it comes to parties and boys.

Problem number two: the so-called "entertainment" has gotta be fun *for guys* too. That rules out doing a '50s fashion show or showing all the *Anne of Green Gables* videos back to back . . . maybe Matt's idea of touch football wasn't so far off, after all!

Oh, man . . . what am I gonna do?!

— *Click!* —

Called Kimberly . . . she didn't know boys had been invited either! But she suggested playing dumb and telling our parents *after* the party. After all . . . we honestly didn't know when we first asked 'em, right?

Guess I'll sleep on it . . . I'm too tired to think anymore, anyway. At least I got the first draft of my English essay done . . . that gives me time to edit it and print it out tomorrow night—*after* I get home from the mall. Kimberly and I are going shopping after school tomorrow to buy Cristan's birthday presents. Wish I had the money to replace the vest I totaled in the clothes dryer . . . but guess that'll just have to wait.

G'night, E.D.

— *Click!* —

P.S. . . . idea! Maybe I should ask George or Bobby for some party ideas that guys would like . . . besides watching "Wrestling Mania" or something dorky like that.

Only prob . . . I don't know if they've been invited. If they haven't, asking them to suggest ideas for Cristan's party could be a major blooper! . . . Guess I could kinda fish around and ask George what he's doin' Friday night . . . but if he says "nothin'," *then* what do I say? . . . or I could ask Cristan who's on her guest list . . . arrrrggh! WHY does life have to be so complicated?!

— Click! —

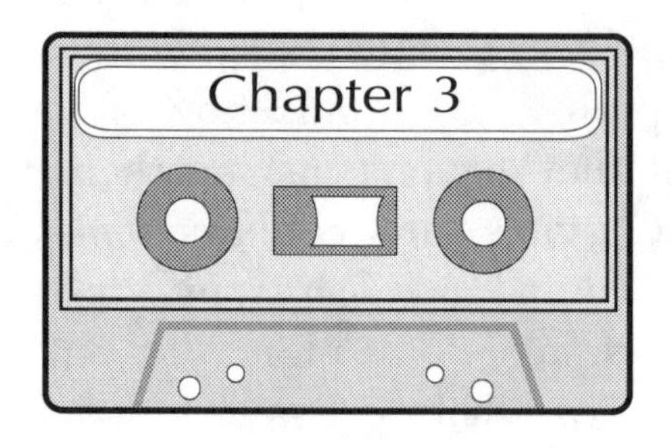

Mannequin Mania

I got it! I got it, E.D.! The greatest idea since roller blading. And YOU, my electronic wonder diary, are going to be the star of the show—I mean, party!

You see . . . well, let me back up and tell you how it happened.

Okay, it's Thursday . . . and I'm recording this after dinner on Day 4,859 in the unfolding drama known as Drea Thomas' Secret Adventures. Countdown: Day Two until Cristan's party. I didn't babysit the Long kids today, so right after school Kimberly and I caught the bus to the mall. Of course we had to stop by the Sugar Bun Counter and get a mammoth cinnamon roll each—ya know, the ones big enough to feed a family of four or one famished teenager, with warm drippy icing that gets all over your fingers, your face, and your favorite saddle shoes. Then we wasted half an hour in the restroom trying to get unsticky.

We finally got serious about getting our gifts for Cristan and headed for the Toy Barn and Just Jewels. Cristan collects stuffed animals, and I'd seen a cute black-and-white penguin with a red bow tie the last time I took Matt and Rebecca to the Toy Barn. She also got her ears pierced last year, so earrings were another hot item on our list.

On the way, however, guess who we bumped into, E.D.? Bobby Wilson and George Easton! 'Course they're a little hard to miss, even in a crowd. They look like junior high versions of the black and white basketball duo in "White Men Can't Jump" . . . except their sport is soccer and they started out as best friends, not rivals.

Anyway, George said, "Yo, Drea . . . hi, Kimberly. You guys got any gift ideas for Cristan's birthday party?"

Kimberly and I looked at each other and burst out laughing. So they were invited after all! I felt really relieved. At least I'd know *some* of the boys coming to this party.

We suggested a cassette tape or CD of Cristan's fav music group—that seemed safe for a guy to give a girl. I didn't exactly admit this, but I don't think I'd want George giving Cristan earrings or a stuffed animal. That seems too . . . too personal, don't you think, E.D.?

Anyway. We said good-bye and started out once more for the Toy Barn, and on the way we "just happened" to pass Flashions—our fav store for clothes—and stopped to look in the windows. A mannequin wearing a multicolored knit hat with a wide floppy brim caught my eye, and I almost changed my mind about the penguin . . . what a *great* hat! I was drooling over the hat, and didn't notice at first that the mannequin didn't have any other clothes on!

Then I realized that a store clerk was changing the outfits on several mannequins. I'd never seen anyone actually change window displays before, and I wondered how the mannequins felt about this "downside" of their modeling job . . . standing there in public with no clothes on, where the whole world could stare at them . . .

And then I heard, "What are you staring at, Nosey?"—it was the mannequin with The Hat and she was staring right at me! With one deft motion, the mannequin stretched out a skinny arm, lifted a big bath towel from a display shelf, and did a neat body wrap.

"Uh . . . I, uh, was just admiring your hat," I said, flashing an innocent smile. At least a towel

was better than trying to talk to a bare mannequin.

"Well, don't," grumbled the mannequin. "How would you feel if people stared at you all day? Never a moment to yourself . . . even when you have to change clothes. Do the store clerks ever consider OUR feelings? Did anybody ever ask me if I wanted to wear this stupid hat?"

"Oh, but that's a great hat," I assured her.

"Easy for you to say," said the mannequin. "You obviously like hats . . . and not just hats, but crazy hats—if that strange creation on your head can be called a hat."

"Now, just a minute," I protested, taking off the green knit crush hat I was wearing and looking at it affectionately. "This little number just happened to be my grandmother's favorite—and I'm carrying on the grand tradition of the Thirties into the Nineties."

"Whatever," sniffed the mannequin. "At least you have a choice. Me . . . I'd rather wear evening gowns and pearls than floppy hats and short skirts and baggy blouses that seem to be the rage these days."

This was amazing. It had never occurred to me that the mannequins might like to have a say in what they modeled in the windows. "Yeah, but think of all the fab clothes you get to wear, something different every season," I said encouragingly. "Flashions has all the best clothes."

"Well," said the mannequin, batting her painted eyelashes, "you try being a mannequin for a day and see how you like it . . ."

"What are you mumbling about?" Kimberly said, interrupting my Secret Adventure into mannequin land. "C'mon . . . we're supposed to be shopping for Cristan."

But right then my mind wasn't on gift buying. "Kimberly," I said thoughtfully, "did you ever stop to think what it would be like to be a mannequin? . . . with people staring at you all day . . . and having to hold the same pose all the time?"

Kimberly was giving me one of her what-on-earth-are-you-talking-about looks. But I ignored her, because something else had caught my eye: the store clerk had disappeared from the display window, leaving the little doorway between the window and the store open. I quickly glanced through the main door into the store, and saw that the clerk had walked back to the manager's desk and was using the telephone.

On the spur of the moment I said to Kimberly,

"Wait here a minute," and dashed into the store. It only took two seconds to find the open panel that led into the store window. Without stopping to think—if I had, I might have gotten cold feet!—I stepped into the store window and struck a pose: head to the side, arms and hands held at weird angles.

Out of the corner of my eye I could see Kimberly looking into the main doorway with a frustrated look. A couple people passed by the Flashions windows without even glancing in. Then a mother and her little boy wandered by and stopped . . . and suddenly, even through the window glass, I heard the little boy say, "Mommy, is that statue real?" . . . and he was pointing right at me!

Kimberly was frowning impatiently, but she glanced in the direction the boy was pointing—and her chin nearly dropped off.

"Drea Thomas," she mouthed at me in silent fury, "you get out of that window right this minute, or I'll . . . I'll . . ."

A couple other people had stopped and were looking puzzled. Then I waved my right hand in one short, quick motion, like a robot, and the little boy went ballistic. "That statue moved! I saw her! She moved her hand! Did you see, Mommy? Did you see?" he screamed.

I guess the mother hadn't seen me move, because she was looking embarrassed and pulling on the little boy's arm to get him to leave.

Out of the corner of my eye, I saw the clerk who'd been dressing the mannequins starting back my way and thought, *I'm outta here!* But I couldn't hold my laughter back any longer. Ducking out of the window holding my sides, I rejoined Kimberly, who looked as if she wanted to have me arrested by the crazy police.

She grabbed my arm and sped me down the mall. "What on earth were you doing in there?" she hissed at me after we'd passed a couple more stores.

I was laughing so hard I could hardly answer. "I just wanted to know what it felt like to be a mannequin," I said. "Really . . . the looks on people's faces when this 'mannequin' moved!"

"Well, next time you want to know what it feels like to be a . . . a mannequin, or . . . or a policewoman . . . or a taxi driver," Kimberly fumed, "you take that Walkman of yours and *ask* them—you don't have to actually *do* it!"

And that, E.D., is what gave me the most fantastic idea for Cristan's party.

"That's it!" I cried, grabbing Kimberly and whirling her around in front of Imports Unlimited.

"Drea, are you losing your mind?" she gasped. "Whatever are you talking about?"

"That's what we're going to do for Cristan's birthday party! We're going to have an *audio* scavenger hunt . . . you know, dividing up into teams, and giving each team a Walkman, and then finding people like a policeman or a taxi driver or a librarian . . . or even a pizza delivery person, or someone over eighty . . . and asking them *on tape* some crazy questions! And the first team to interview everyone on their list wins!"

Kimberly just stared at me for . . . must have been a million seconds. Then she just said, "The mannequin, too?"

Which cracked us up, and we could hardly stop laughing long enough pick out a pair of big, dangly, silver earrings at Just Jewels (from Kimberly) and the black-and-white penguin at the Toy Barn (from me) before it was time to catch our bus . . . and then we had to run the entire length of the mall to make it in time.

But just as we passed Flashions again, Kimberly screeched to a stop and pointed at a big sign that someone had put up in the window since . . . well, since I'd tried being a mannequin. It said, "FLASHIONS ONCE-A-YEAR SALE! 50%-75% off all merchandise! This Saturday ONLY!"

We both looked at each other. Fifty to seventy-five percent off! This was too good to be true! I had bought the vest I ruined at Flashions—now maybe I could get one to replace it!

"Oh, wait a minute," I said. "I just spent my last dime on Cristan's penguin . . . and my big weekend baby-sitting the Long kids isn't until next week."

"But doesn't Mrs. Long pay you on Friday each week for the after school stuff?" Kimberly asked.

I perked up. She was right. It wouldn't be as much money as I'll get for the upcoming weekend—but it might be enough to get another vest.

Isn't it just too wild for words, E.D.? Within the space of half an hour, I got my idea for Cristan's party "entertainment" . . . we found the perfect birthday gifts . . . *and* we bumped into the sale of the year at our favorite store! What a weekend this is going to be!

Oh, man . . . look at the time! I better get that English essay finished and study for my integers test. Then I gotta call George and Bobby and a couple of other kids and see if I can borrow several more Walkmans.

— Click! —

Oh. Forgot to say that I decided to tell Mom and Dad about Cristan inviting boys to her party this year. Like Grandpa said, they give me responsibilities because they trust me . . . so here goes. But if they say no, I'm in BIG trouble with Kimberly and Cristan.

Wish me luck, E.D.

— Click! —

Yes! Mom and Dad really liked my idea for the audio scavenger hunt . . . 'course Dad asked questions about where we'd go, how we were going to get there, how long we'd be out, and all that Dad sort of stuff . . . but when I told him about George and Bobby and some other guys being invited, he was actually relieved! He thought it was safer being out in groups of guys and girls than just girls alone. Mom suggested we do our scavenger hunt at the mall—more security guards around, I guess—and I agreed on 9:30 being the back-at-Cristan's time, and that was all.

Sometimes parents can be really amazing—and weird. Now they've decided to both wallpaper *and* paint the dining room in a marathon redecorating sprint all this weekend.

I'm glad I'm gonna be outta here! Otherwise Mom and Dad would have suckered me into helping them redo the entire house!

— Click! —

This Little Pig Went to Drea's House

It's Day 4,860 . . . time: eighteen hundred and forty-five hours—that's 6:45 p.m. to the uninitiated . . . and I'm up in my attic room waiting for Kimberly to arrive.

What a week, E.D.! But I think I got everything done . . . except my school art project, which may need to be titled, "Unfinished."

As for the countdown: In exactly fifteen minutes my weekend shifts into high gear when Kimberly and I leave to attend the "Mother of All Birthday Parties" at Cristan Canter's house. My gift is wrapped . . . and I talked George Easton into rounding up the other Walkmans for the audio scavenger hunt . . . oh, yeah. George thinks the audio scavenger hunt idea is "awesome" . . . that's his exact word.

Anyway, I think I'm all ready—even without the vest I'd planned to wear. I've got on my flowered tapestry vest instead . . . so, as usual, I will make an absolutely ravishing entrance! In fact, I wonder what it would be like to model a line of my own clothes, E.D. . . .

Here I am, Drea the Famous Fashion Model striking a pose, an amused smile on my lips. I hear the cameras click . . .

"Arch those eyebrows! Lower those eyelids!" yells the photographer. Hmm, how do I do that? I wonder. But up goes an eyebrow . . . down go the eyelids. Ah . . . the bored look . . .

"No, no, it's all wrong for Drea," my fashion agent protests. "Drea isn't a sultry French model. She's . . . she's fresh! She's energetic! Be yourself, Drea . . . move!"

So I drop the fake "pout" and flash my amazing grin. I can almost feel my eyes twinkle. I pull my hat down mischievously . . .

The cameras click, click, click . . .

Quick! A clothes change . . . then an-

other . . . the makeup lady gives a quick powder to my face . . .

The photographer's shouting directions: "Move!" "Hold still!" Click . . . click . . . click . . .

"Fantastic!" cries the photographer.

"What did I tell you?" sniffs my agent. "Drea Thomas is the newest teen fashion sensation . . ."

Oh! Uh . . . Hi, Kimberly! How did you get up here without me hearing you? . . . Yeah, I'm ready . . . I know, I know . . . "let's jet."

— *Click!* —

You will never believe this, E.D. I can hardly believe it myself . . . in fact, I'm still in shock.

You see, Kimberly and I were dashing out of the house—our friend Chenille's mom was gonna pick us up—and I just stopped by Disaster City (meaning the dining room) to say good-bye to Mom and Dad, who were up to their eyeballs in ladders and paint and wallpaper. Mom had her hair pulled back in a pony tail and looked about eighteen . . .

"Mom, we're gone!" I said, being a Dutiful Daughter and letting them know that I was off to the party.

Dad couldn't resist one last jab. "Hey," he said, "don't you want to stick around and redecorate the dining room with your *swell* parents?"

E.D., nobody but parents who grew up in the

Jurassic Age says "swell" anymore, but . . . it kinda went with the baseball cap and suspenders and paint smocks.

"That's very funny, Mr. Thomas," said Kimberly sweetly.

"Dad . . . be real," I said.

Mom waved her paint roller at us and said, "We've got a couple more paint smocks in the closet, if you girls really want to, uh, 'paint the town.'"

I smiled patiently. "Gee, that's *swell,* Mom, but . . . we're outta here!"

And Kimberly and I beat a hasty exit.

"Did anybody ever tell you that your parents are weird?" Kimberly asked me.

Right. She's mentioned it once or twice . . . like every time she comes over.

We headed for the back door, Cristan's birthday gifts in hand. "I just can't wait until somebody we know gets a driver's license," Kimberly said. "Then we won't have to always have one of our Moms pick us uuuuupp—"

As Kimberly pulled the back door open, she stopped suddenly, and I crashed into her. I peeked around her shoulder, ready to give her a ticket for reckless walking . . . and looked right into the face of Mrs. Long, who had her hand held up in a fist, as if she'd just been about to knock at our door.

Then I looked down, and there stood Rebecca and Matt Long, loaded down with backpacks and pillows, grinning up at me.

Kimberly recovered first. "Mrs. Long!" she said, as if she ran into our principal at my back door every Friday evening.

Mrs. Long smiled. "Perfect timing! Here they are, Drea, ready for a weekend with their favorite baby-sitter! Okay, guys . . ." she said, marching Rebecca and Matt past us and into the kitchen.

That's when it hit me—HARD—right between the eyes. *It must be THIS weekend—NOT next weekend—that I'm supposed to baby-sit the Long kids!* In one slow-motion second, I saw my whole weekend disappearing in a SNAP.

Mrs. Long looked at me with concern. "Drea? Is something wrong?" she asked.

"Oh, no . . . no," I said numbly, as I picked my jaw off the floor. "Everything's . . . uh, just fine."

Kimberly was staring at me, her mouth open in an I-don't-believe-this look. She hit her hand to her forehead and muttered, "Yeah. Everything's great. It's gonna be a howl."

As if on cue, we heard a mournful whine, followed by an impatient bark, outside the door.

I'd forgotten about Floyd.

Floyd pushed open the back door, galloped into the kitchen, jumped up on my chest and planted a sloppy dog kiss right on my face. Eewwwww.

"Nice to see you, too, Floyd," I said, wiping my face with the back of my hand.

Matt grabbed Floyd's collar and pulled him off me before I dissolved in dog slobber. "Floyd is really excited to be here," he explained with seven-year-old wisdom. "He hates the kennel."

"But he loves *you*, Drea," Rebecca piped up.

"I can't imagine why," I muttered . . .

Hmm. I wondered what I looked like through Floyd's eyes . . . or nose. Dogs are famous for their noses . . . and Floyd certainly has a big one—just like the rest of him! Maybe to him, I smell like the ultimate in canine desire—like some new, delicious scent called "Dog Biscuit Perfume" . . . and like any other self-respecting dog, if it smells good, you slobber on it!

Oops. Sorry for that little detour, E.D. These things just pop into my head. Anyway . . . back to my tale of woe.

Mrs. Long and the kids were so cheerful, I don't think they noticed that Kimberly and I were in a state of shock. "Here's the address and phone number for the hotel in Philadelphia where the School Principals Conference is being held," Mrs. Long said, handing me a piece of paper. Then she turned to the kids. "Now, Matt, Rebecca, don't forget . . .

Floyd is your responsibility, okay? Matt, where is Floyd's duffel bag?"

This was too much for Kimberly. "Floyd has a *duffel bag*?"

Sure enough. Floyd had a duffel bag, which Matt proceeded to open and list its contents: "It's all in here. Floyd's bowl . . . Floyd's food . . . Floyd's bone . . . Floyd's pig . . ."

And out came the weirdest, pink, rubber toy, with a pig head held up by a long, wobbly neck. It went, "Squeaky, squeaky," when Matt squeezed.

There was a flurry of good-byes and kisses and hugs, then Mrs. Long disappeared with a breezy, "Gotta run! See you Sunday!" . . . and there we were: two dismayed partygoers, two eager baby-sittees, one extremely large, slobbery dog, and one strange rubber pig—all staring at each other.

A car horn outside brought us back to reality.

"That's Chenille and her mom!" Kimberly said desperately. "You've gotta come. Now!"

For a brief second I thought about palming the whole gig off on my parents for the evening . . . but I knew it would never fly.

My "responsibility" was staring up at me with two pairs of blue eyes and freckles.

"I can't go," I sighed. "Matt, Rebecca . . . you guys take your stuff upstairs. Take Floyd, too—but only in my room."

When they were gone, Kimberly really turned

on the steam. "Let me get this straight," she fumed. "This is the most incredible weekend of our lives . . . and you're going to spend it with two rug rats, a giant drooling mop with paws, and . . . and a dorky rubber pig?!"

I just shrugged—but I swear, E.D., that pig stretched its long, rubbery neck and winked at me.

Kimberly wasn't through yet. "There's got to be a way out," she said. "I know . . . have the kids go to bed early."

Yeah, right. Like it was only seven o'clock.

By this time I was accepting the inevitable. So I handed Cristan's present to Kimberly and said, "Guess I'll see you Monday . . . I'm responsible for these kids all weekend."

Kimberly stared at me incredulously. "You have a responsibility to your friends, too, you know," she said. "Don't you read the latest research?"

Sometimes Kimberly drives me nuts. I didn't have a clue what she was talking about. But she was about to tell me whether I wanted to hear it or not.

"Teenagers today are *supposed* to be totally self-centered and self-absorbed," she said matter-of-factly. "Adults expect this of us! You can't start going around being responsible . . . especially with your own principal's kids."

The car horn blasted once more, and Kimberly, thoroughly disgusted, opened the back door. "This is going to cause some serious grief to the rest of us who are completely and happily irresponsible!" she said . . . then added sarcastically, "Thanks a lot."

As if I had planned it this way on purpose!

That was 7:02. At 7:03 Mom walked in, mumbling, "Primer . . . base coat . . . first coat . . . second coat . . . it's going to be a long weekend."

My mom, the prophet. "Longer than you know," I sighed.

That's when we heard barking from the attic.

"Funny . . . I didn't know Kimberly could bark like a dog," my mom said absently. Obviously, she didn't have a clue what had just happened.

"Hey, Mom," I said, trying to break the news gently, "remember when you said I could baby-sit Matt and Rebecca over the weekend?"

She gave me a look. "I thought . . . next weekend."

I nodded. "So did I. But it turns out I was wrong—it's *this* weekend. And, uh, I forgot to mention . . ." —The barking upstairs was getting more rambunctious— ". . . Floyd."

The truth dawned on my mom. "Ah. I see. Uh . . . remind me again, how big is Floyd?"

I waved my hand vaguely in the air. "Oh . . . just a little taller than Matt."

Mom's eyes glazed over. I could tell there wasn't room for this information in her brain, along with two shades of green paint, wallpaper, and wallpaper paste. "Well." She smiled diplomatically . . . the way I've seen her smile at a difficult client at

Jamison's department store. "Well. Just keep everybody and everything out of the dining room, okay, Honey?" And she escaped back into the dining room—to break the news to my dad, I guess.

It's now 7:15, E.D., and I've spent the last ten minutes crying on your electronic "shoulder." But the noises upstairs are getting louder. Guess I better make a quick call to Cristan's house and ask George if he'll organize and lead the audio scavenger hunt . . . hope he has enough Walkmans without you, E.D. I have a feeling your batteries are gonna get a workout around *here* this weekend.

As for this . . . this pig . . . make yourself at home, Squeaky . . .

I picked up Floyd's pink pig and squeezed it a couple times—"Squeaky! Squeaky!" Then I set it down again . . . and I swear that pig stretched out its long, wobbly neck and took a humongous bite out of an apple in the fruit basket! Some pigs take things literally!

Sigh. But maybe things can't get any worse than they are already . . . right, E.D.?

Over and out.

— *Click!* —

The Dining Room Gets "Redecorated"

What was that I said a couple hours ago, E.D.? "Things can't get any worse than they are already—right?"

Right. Famous last words.

It's now nine o'clock and I'm already in bed, wrapped in flannel down to my ankles . . . while somewhere out in Hampton Falls, twenty kids—no, make that nineteen—are running around the mall with Walkmans interviewing cops and taxi drivers and security guards, having a blast on *my* audio scavenger hunt.

But that's not the worst of it, E.D.

Ya see, when I got up to my attic room, Matt was playing ball with Floyd, and had gotten him all excited. As I came in the door, Matt and Rebecca jumped all over me.

"What are we gonna do all weekend?"

"How 'bout the zoo?"

"No, no . . . the park!"

In self-defense, I sputtered, "Maybe a nice, quiet nature walk instead . . . ?"

At that point, Floyd went bananas. He bounced up onto my bed, then off again, wagging his rear end in a frantic dance. Matt grabbed him and tried to calm him down.

"Don't use the 'W' word around Floyd," Rebecca warned me.

"You mean 'wal—'" I started to say, but both Matt and Rebecca waved their hands frantically.

"No, no! That word makes him crazy," said Rebecca.

Matt nodded. "He's very sensitive, you know."

I tried to keep a straight face. (Matt was *so* serious!) So I said, "Okay. We'll plan something fun in the morning. Why don't you guys get ready now for your baths—"

And suddenly Floyd went bananas again . . . tearing around my room in a gray and white blur, scattering floor pillows, crashing into my night table, bumping into my bookcase and sending books tumbling, his ears and long hair flying. . . .

"What did I say now?" I cried, as Matt and Rebecca dived for Floyd and tried to grab his collar.

"THE 'B' WORD!" they both yelled at me.

Just then Floyd slipped through their hands and made a dash for the door leading downstairs.

"Secure all exits!" I yelled. "Block off the stairs!"

Rebecca valiantly planted her body in front of the open doorway leading downstairs—but Floyd noticed the other door leading into the rest of the attic was open a crack, did a fast ninety degrees, and pushed through the attic door. A moment later we heard loud thuds as boxes crashed to the floor.

Matt, Rebecca, and I ran after Floyd into the attic, but it was dark, and we kept bumping into each other. Then I felt something hairy brush past me . . . Floyd! But before I could grab, he was gone, thudding and crashing into something else. Then I saw him again, heading back into my room.

Without thinking, I grabbed my old butterfly net and headed after him. But by the time I got into my room, all I saw of Floyd was his rear end . . . disappearing down the stairs!

"Oh, no-o-o!" I wailed, dropped the net, and clattered down the stairs after him, with Matt and Rebecca on my heels.

I'm not quite sure what happened next, E.D., but Floyd led us on a merry chase all the way to the first floor, then around and around the kitchen table. After a while the room started spinning, so I slowed down . . . but then Floyd skidded into the pantry, and all three of us ran after him, thinking we had him cornered . . . but somehow he slipped right through our legs and ran right back out again into the kitchen, straight through the swinging door into the . . . right, you guessed it.

Straight into the dining room.

A strange yell pierced the swinging door. Something like, "Yeeooww!" I think it was my dad . . . followed by several loud thumps and a ghastly cry. I think that one was my mom.

I just stood paralyzed in the kitchen, holding onto Matt and Rebecca, whose eyes were as wide as a night owl's.

Then, out came Floyd, trotting straight toward us, with a funny green stripe down his back. As if on cue, all three of us tackled the dog, this time getting a good grip on his collar. Floyd sat down as if he was suddenly tired of the game.

There were no more sounds from the dining room. For about two seconds, that is. Then the door was flung open by two very strange creatures . . . one resembled my dad, except one half of him was plastered with a long strip of wallpaper from his head down to his ankles. The other creature was completely unrecognizable . . . hair, face, and shirt all dripping the same, wet, solid, green color—sorta like pictures I used to draw of Martians landing in space ships. Only this 'Martian' was . . . well, uh, to put it mildly . . . shaking with anger.

But the voices that spoke in unison definitely

belonged to Mom and Dad. "OUT!" they sputtered, pointing shaking fingers first at Floyd, then at the back door.

My mouth was dry; I couldn't say a thing. So I just prodded Matt, who took Floyd by the collar and proceeded to shuffle toward the back door . . . looking as if Floyd had just been banished to Siberia. Matt looked mournfully back at my dad, who managed to keep frowning and looking firm, even as the wallpaper started to peel off his face.

So we took Floyd out into the backyard, found a long piece of rope in the garden shed, and tied him up outside. The back door opened behind us and Dad called out, "And you better wash that paint off Floyd before it dries!" Then the door slammed.

Matt looked like he was about to cry.

"Floyd will be all right," I assured him. "It doesn't get very cold at night yet . . . and Floyd's got a thick, warm coat."

The kids were amazingly quiet the rest of the evening. They each took a bath, got into their p.j.'s and robes, and read some books. When I came out of the bathroom in my robe, Matt was playing with a flashlight, making shadow pictures with his fingers on the wall.

"What's that supposed to be?" asked Rebecca, gawking at the jerky shadow on the wall.

"It's Floyd," Matt said, in a can't-you-tell voice.

"Huh. It looks more like a tree tripping over a

pair of scissors," said Rebecca.

Where was her imagination? Didn't she know that, by squinting just so, it looked exactly like Floyd? Well . . . on second thought, not exactly. In fact, to be honest, not even close. So, I thought I'd help Matt out with a little imagination . . .

I looked slyly at Matt, then back at the wall. The jerky shadow suddenly danced to life, as a perfect silhouette of an English sheepdog, long hair flowing, bounded around and around the circumference of the flashlight's beam on the wall.

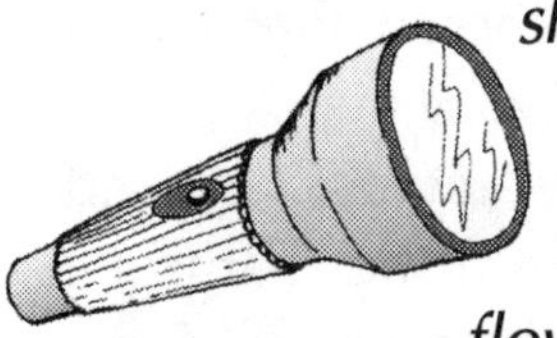

Matt grinned at me. "Cool, Drea!" he said. "Can you make a giant Ultrasaurus fighting a Stegosaurus?"

"He's into dinosaurs," Rebecca explained with exaggerated big-sister patience.

It's a little awesome realizing that certain kids can "see" my imagination. But there *are* limits. "Ahh," I backed out, "that's a little complicated . . . I think it's time for bed. Did everybody say their prayers?"

The sad look returned to Matt's face. "I prayed

that Floyd will be safe outside tonight."

I assured both kids that Floyd was going to be just fine and told them to go to sleep. But . . . I'm a little worried, too. Hmm. Maybe I should go down and check on him. Be back in a minute, E.D. . . .

— Click! —

Back again. Everything's okay. I didn't exactly go out and check on the dog, but I heard my parents talking in the kitchen, and I gathered that Floyd was okay.

When I got to the bottom of the stairs, I peeked around the corner and saw Mom in her bathrobe holding a cup of hot tea. Her hair was wrapped in a towel, so I guess she got all that paint out. Dad was sitting at the kitchen table, muttering something about having to go to the hardware store in the morning and get more wallpaper . . . and more paint and more paste and a new brush.

Even from the stairs I could hear Floyd whimpering out in the yard, and my mom actually said, "Poor thing."

Dad said, "Oh, it's all right. I'll survive . . . " before he realized she was talking about the dog!

I wanted to giggle but decided my parents weren't laughing about the situation quite yet.

Mom opened the back door and looked out. "Floyd looks so sad out there," she said sympathetically.

"Not half as sad as our dining room looks," my dad reminded her.

At that point Mom called out firmly, "Sorry, Floyd, but you're going to have to spend the night outside, fella. Goodnight."

So, I guess he's okay . . . just lonely.

And frankly, E.D., it's a little hard to work up a lot of sympathy for Floyd. He may have to sleep outside tonight, but yours truly is talking to her electronic diary at 9:30 on a Friday night, while Kimberly, George, Bobby, Cristan and the rest of the gang are probably wrapping up a wildly successful audio scavenger hunt—my idea, no less—eating pizza-with-the-works and Cristan's mother's famous cherry cheesecake.

Woe and gloom.

— Click! —

Oh, no! I forgot to wash that paint off Floyd's back. Uhh . . . what time is it? Oh, groan . . . 10:15 . . . I really *don't* want to get dressed and go outside and give that big mutt a bath in the dark. I'll do it first thing tomorrow morning.

G'night, E.D. This time for real.

— Click! —

Famous Last Words . . . Times Three

Day 4,861, Saturday morning . . . time: oh-ten-hundred hours . . . in the Catastrophic Adventures of Drea Thomas. I thought it couldn't get much worse than the Dining Room Disaster last night . . . but it has.

It all started with breakfast, E.D.

When Rebecca and I came downstairs in our bathrobes—I think it was about 8:15—Matt was already up and sitting at the kitchen table. He didn't say much, but I didn't really notice at the time . . . I was still feeling pretty awful about the Dining Room Disaster.

"Mom," I said, "I'm really sorry about the mess. I'll pay for all of the damage out of my baby-sitting money."

She gave me an odd look, as if to say, "Do you really want to be in debt until you're ninety three?" But all she actually said was, "Oh, well . . . thank you, Honey. But don't worry about it. Sometimes these things just happen." Then she made a face. "Luckily, your father has always liked me in green."

I couldn't *believe* she was making a joke about it!

But both Mom and Dad seemed in good spirits this morning. They both were dressed in casual pants and sport tops, and if I didn't know better, no one would guess that just last night my father had been plastered with wallpaper paste and my mother covered in green paint.

Dad propelled Mom out the door. "We're going to the hardware store to restock the supplies for our next assault on the dining room renovation," he informed us. "C'mon, Laurie . . . Hold the fort, kids," he said, giving a mock salute. "We shall return!"

Kimberly is right. My parents really are weird . . . in a nice kind of way.

Anyway . . . I felt a little better knowing that my baby-sitting money wasn't going to be docked for the next trillion years. "Okay, you guys," I said to Rebecca and Matt. "What do you want for breakfast?"

"Pancakes," said Matt.

"Waffles," said Rebecca.

They glared at each other.

"Pancakes!"

"Waffles!"

That settled it: it was eggs and toast for everybody. While the kids set the table, I dropped some toast into the toaster, who as usual had his own opinion . . .

"So!" Mr. Toaster said brightly. "What's on the social calendar for today?"

I shrugged and leaned on the counter. "I dunno yet. Got any suggestions?"

The toaster nodded with excitement. "The automatic toaster is seventy-five years old this year, and I hear there's quite an anniversary bash at the Charles Strite Museum . . . he invented the electric toaster, you know."

Ask a stupid question . . . get a stupid answer. "Are you unplugged?" I said. "We need something that's exciting for HUMANS."

The toaster gave a big "Humph!" and looked offended. But I pretended not to notice and opened the refrigerator to get out some eggs.

But the eggs saw me coming, and two of them made a break for the back of the refrigerator shelf, disappearing somewhere behind all those cartons and bottles.

"Awright," I muttered, "I'm gonna find you guys!" It was bad enough having Mr. Toaster make stupid suggestions without the eggs going on strike.

"They're behind the milk! . . . behind the milk!" the toaster tattled.

I moved the milk carton and sure enough: there were the two egg-scapees, hiding in the corner at the back of the refrigerator, laughing at how flustered I was getting. But the jig was up: I reached in, wrapped my hand around their slippery little shells and brought them out to the counter.

The toaster cackled gleefully. "Ha, ha, ha . . . you guys are cracked!"

And that's exactly what I did: cracked those eggs into a bowl and scrambled 'em!

But while the kitchen was conspiring to make my morning difficult, E.D., the real drama was about to break. Matt filled Floyd's bowl with water and took it outside . . . two seconds later we heard him shriek, "Floyd? . . . Floyd? . . . Oh, no! Floyd is gone!

It was true. Floyd was missing!

I was *sure* I tied that rope tight last night. But the rope was just lying there as if someone had untied him. I'm sure he's a valuable dog. What if . . . Oh, no, E.D.! What if someone dognapped him?

Matt and Rebecca and I looked all over the yard and in the garden shed and garage and in the neighbors' yards, but . . . no Floyd. Mom and Dad had already left for the hardware store, so they couldn't help us find him.

So right now I'm waiting for George to show up on his bike and help us hunt for him. I called Kimberly, too, but her mom said she had already left for the Flashions once-a-year sale . . . which, by the way, I am missing—another calamity I am NOT going to think about.

Sure wish George would hurry up . . . what's that, Rebecca? Sorry . . . I was talking to my electronic diary and didn't hear what you said . . .

— *Click!* —

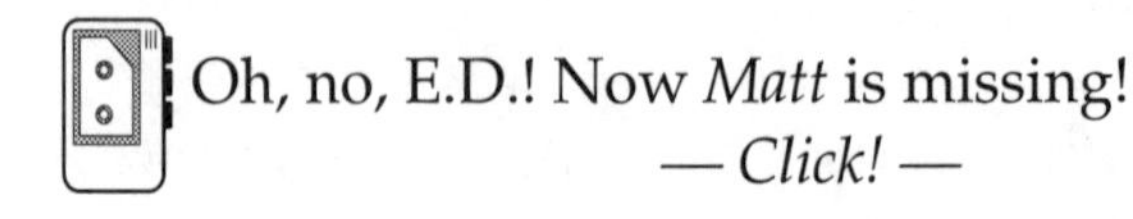

Oh, no, E.D.! Now *Matt* is missing!

— *Click!* —

I'm back again, E.D., and it's now Saturday afternoon . . . but this morning I think I survived the two most scary hours of my life.

I thought this responsibility thing would be a piece of cake. That was *before* yesterday. A couple hours ago all I could think of was Mrs. Long coming back Sunday night and me having to say, "Oh, sure, Mrs. Long, I know I said I'd take care of your kids and your dog while you were out of town . . . but I lost the dog, and . . . oh, yes, I lost your son, too. Sorry 'bout that."

By the time George arrived to help look for Floyd, I was frantic. *Both* Floyd and Matt were lost!

George took off on his bike in one direction, and Rebecca and I went on foot in the other. We must have asked a zillion and a half people if they'd seen a big gray and white English sheepdog the size of a small car or a short boy with a baseball cap and a blue shirt . . . but we might as well have been asking if they'd seen a little green Martian with a pet caterpillar.

Then suddenly Rebecca and I saw a little kid across the park wearing a blue baseball cap with a red brim. We ran like crazy and practically tackled him . . . but it wasn't Matt, and we probably scared the poor kid to death.

George came riding up about then with the same story: no one had seen a big hairy pooch or a cute lost seven-year-old.

I was pretty discouraged—maybe even a little scared—and had no idea what to do next. "You don't think he got all the way downtown, do you?" I asked.

George shrugged. "I hope not," he said, "but . . . we'd better check it out."

I watched him ride off again. What a guy . . . it made me feel better just knowing he was on the case. One of the things I like best about George is his loyalty. He's somebody you can count on . . . and I knew he wouldn't quit till we'd found 'em both.

Rebecca gave a big sigh. "Matt really got himself lost this time."

I looked at her. "*This* time?"

"Yeah," she said. "Once he got lost in the supermarket. But he climbed up to the top of the cookie shelves on Aisle Nine until he saw Mom over on Aisle Four. He's a pretty smart kid, for a little brother."

Which is what gave me the idea of how to find Matt. I grabbed Rebecca's hand and started running back into the park.

"What are we doing?" Rebecca cried, probably thinking I'd finally flipped.

"We've been looking *around* for Matt," I cried. "It's time to start looking *up*."

We ran from tree to tree in the park, looking up into the leafy branches. Suddenly Rebecca yelled,

"Over there! Look!"

There in the crook of a large oak tree was a small figure acting like a lookout on top of a ship's mast.

"Matt!" we screamed. Sure enough, as we ran closer, we could see Matt waving back at us.

"I thought we'd lost you!" I croaked, as he slid down the trunk of the tree.

"Oh, I'm not lost," he said cheerfully. "I'm right here."

Rebecca rolled her eyes in a "spare me!" look.

"Matt," I scolded, "don't ever run away like that without telling me where you're going. I was really worried."

He hung his head and said, "I'm sorry, Drea."

"Why did you run off like that?" I demanded.

Matt's voice quavered. "Well, it's all my fault that Floyd ran away," he said.

"Your fault?" I asked. "What do you mean?"

That's when he admitted that he had snuck outside in the middle of the night and brought Floyd into the kitchen. I guess the two of them slept all night right on the kitchen floor . . . until this morning when he heard my parents getting up and clunking down the stairs toward the kitchen. Afraid of getting caught, Matt just pushed Floyd out the back door . . . and, well, you know the rest, E.D.

"So . . . what are we going to do about Floyd?" asked Rebecca, being her practical self.

"I'm thinking . . . I'm thinking," I muttered.

"Too bad we don't know what Floyd is thinking," said Matt.

What a brilliant kid. Of course!

"That's a great idea, Matt," I told him. "If we could think like Floyd, maybe we could figure out where Floyd went."

"Uh, oh," grinned Rebecca. "I feel a Secret Adventure coming on . . ."

I just smiled. Yes, it was definitely time for a Secret Adventure . . . a Secret Adventure into the world of doggy types. I looked first at one kid, then the other. Now, if Rebecca and Matt were dogs, I pondered, what kind of dogs would they be . . .?

Matt seemed to read my mind.

"Uh-oh," he said doubtfully. "I don't know about this. What if I get fleas . . .?"

But it was too late. The Secret Adventure had already begun . . .

Super Dogs to the Rescue!

At first it didn't seem like anything had changed. I was still in the middle of the city park, in the middle of Hampton Falls, New Jersey . . . but then I looked around for Matt and Rebecca and wanted to laugh.

Instead of a seven-year-old boy, I saw a cute tan-and-white beagle with floppy ears wearing a blue baseball cap with a red brim. Next to him

was a short-legged bassett hound, long ears dragging the ground, wearing Rebecca's wire-rimmed glasses on her doggy nose.

I gave myself a once-over . . . gee, I was a dog, too, but nothing I could recognize—just a large, brown, nondescript mutt in a floppy denim hat and black vest. And all three of us were engaged in the favorite pastime of all dogs (well, most COMMON pastime, anyway) . . . scratching fleas!

"I knew it . . . I just knew it," muttered Matt the beagle, as the little dog stretched a hind leg forward and gave his front shoulder a good scratching. "Hey, you fleas . . . scat!"

Rebecca the bassett hound sniffed the air experimentally. "Oh! Oh! I smell a cat! Wow . . . so THAT'S what a cat smells like! But . . . how am I supposed to chase a cat with THESE legs." The bassett peered forlornly through her wire-rimmed glasses at her short, stubby legs.

They were SO short, her belly almost scraped the ground.

We all sniffed around. Smells leaped out of the ground and wafted on the air around us . . . another dog had been here recently . . . someone was barbecuing somewhere . . . a human had been lying on the grass . . .

Boy, I thought. A dog's nose could keep us busy all day just sniffing smells and figuring out what they were. But, I reminded myself, we weren't in this Secret Adventure just for the fun of it. We had a job to do.

"Now, remember, Matt and Rebecca," I said, pushing the floppy hat out of my eyes with a front paw, "this is a scientific experiment, and we have to take it very serious—"

But at that very moment, I spied a perfect stick for tossing and tugging and throwing.

"Hey!" I interrupted myself. "A stick! Let's play!" I could feel my whole body wiggling with excitement, as if my tail was wagging the rest me.

"I've got it, Drea!" yelped Matt the beagle, diving for the stick. "Tug-of-war! Let's play tug-of-war! Two against one!"

Rebecca the bassett hound, doing her best to keep her belly from dragging on the ground, joined forces with the beagle and clamped her teeth on one end of the stick as I grabbed the other end. Why hadn't I ever realized how much fun it was to play with a stick before? We pulled and pushed . . . pushed and pulled . . . grunting and snarling in mock battle.

Back and forth went the tug-of-war, until suddenly the stick broke in two, sending the bassett and the beagle head over heels off the grass onto the sidewalk into the path of a baby buggy.

Rebecca scrambled up onto her stubby legs first and peered through her glasses at the on-coming buggy.

"Oh, look! Babies!" she bayed—just like a hound. "I love babies."

"Me, too," I said, romping over to the buggy. At least I was a big mutt and could peek inside.

"I wanna see," yapped Matt, leaping up and falling back in a tangled heap of legs and floppy ears. "I wanna see!"

Just then a woman's voice cut through all our yapping and yelping. "Hey! Get away, you dogs! Shoo!" It must have been the baby's mother, because she flapped her hands at the three of us dogs until we backed off. As we turned away, disappointed, we heard her say to another woman walking with her, "Oh! I hope they don't have fleas!"

Good grief! Didn't she know we just wanted a peek? "C'mon, Matt and Rebecca," I muttered, slinking away from the baby buggy, my tail between my legs. "I guess we know where we're not wanted."

"We didn't mean anything, Drea," said Matt the beagle, his brow wrinkled in a sad frown.

"We just wanted to see the babies," added Rebecca, hanging her head so low she kept tripping on her ears.

"I know," I said. "But that lady treated us like . . . like dogs." I shook my floppy hat sadly. "I wonder if that's how Floyd feels sometimes?"

The three of us—mutt, beagle, and basset hound—walked slowly back into the park . . . when suddenly, behind us, a piercing scream cut into the air.

"Eeeeeek! Help! Help! My baby! Somebody catch my baby!"

Rebecca and Matt and I whirled around just

in time to see the baby buggy rolling all by itself down the hilly sidewalk and picking up speed. Inside the buggy, the baby was sitting up in delight, clapping its hands as the buggy flew past bushes and trees.

I quickly looked at the two smaller dogs. "What would Floyd do?" I asked.

"He'd help!" yelped Matt, and took off running after the buggy on his little beagle legs, with me galloping not far behind. But Rebecca the bassett hound saw something we didn't see at first: a gaping construction hole at the bottom of the hill, just where the sidewalk turned.

Pumping her short legs as fast as she could go, the bassett hound headed for the bottom of the hill. Matt and I saw her screech to a stop and brace herself, a split second before the baby

buggy crashed into her.

The baby screamed with delight as the buggy tipped, wobbled, and careened around the corner . . . where it continued rolling down the sidewalk.

Meanwhile, poor Rebecca, her soft, silky fur covered with dirt, pebbles, and sawdust, was clawing her way paw over paw out of the construction hole where she'd been knocked in.

But the baby buggy was once more picking up speed, as it flew past trees, benches, rocks . . . and then we all gasped with horror. It was heading straight toward the pond.

"Super Beagle to the rescue!" yelped Matt, tearing after the buggy. But just then the buggy hit a ski jump of a bump—great for skateboards but bad for carriages—and flew into the air.

"Wheeeeee!" cried the baby, clapping her hands.

"Eeeeeeeeek!" screamed the mother.

"Ooooooooh!" howled Matt.

With a mighty bound, the beagle leaped for

the buggy, and pushed it safely back onto the path. But Matt overestimated his leap and sailed through the air in a beautiful arc . . . right into the pond with a big splash.

It was a beautiful nosedive . . . right to the bottom. Rebecca and I ran up to the edge of the pond and looked in. We saw Matt sink like a stone, blinking in surprise, probably wondering why everything looked so wet.

Uh-oh. Just then we saw trouble . . . a king-size turtle came swimming along the bottom of the pond to investigate just who was disturbing his underwater nap. I'm sure that turtle had never seen a "fish" with floppy ears, a wiggly nose, four furry legs, and a tail before. But the turtle must have decided that Matt didn't belong in his pond, because he did what any self-respecting turtle would do.

He bit the beagle's tail.

Hard.

The next thing we knew, Matt came shooting like a sky rocket straight up through the water, through the air, and through the branches of a . . . no, make that INTO the overhanging branch of a tree.

BONK!

Poor Matt landed with a thud on the ground

. . . and a knot on his noggin. But when the little beagle shook himself and staggered to his paws, I knew he was all right, so I took off after the baby buggy again. By this time I was panting and puffing, but gradually I began gaining on it.

"Doggie!" squealed the baby happily, reaching out her hands toward me . . . and then I saw it.

The buggy was careening straight toward a big oak tree.

In the tree, I could see Mama Squirrel and Papa Squirrel having a little talk with Junior Squirrel . . . who suddenly starting jumping up and down and pointing in our direction. Even though everything was happening at warp speed, I could almost figure out the conversation going on in pantomime in the oak tree . . .

"Uh—Papa," Junior seemed to say, frantically tapping Papa Squirrel on the shoulder.

"Not now, Junior," said Papa. "Don't try to change the subject. Your Mama and I are trying to talk to you about cleaning up your hole in the tree."

"But, Papa—!"

"Don't interrupt, Junior," scolded Mama Squirrel.

"Okay," shrugged Junior. "I guess it isn't

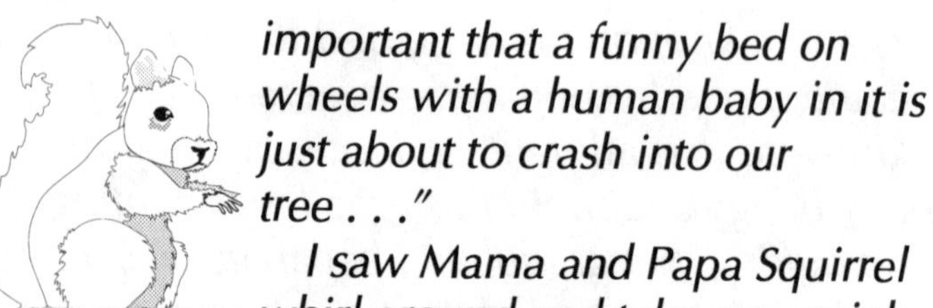

important that a funny bed on wheels with a human baby in it is just about to crash into our tree . . ."

I saw Mama and Papa Squirrel whirl around and take one quick look at the baby buggy hurtling on a collision course with the tree, with a big mutt—me—chasing after it, followed by an hysterical mother screaming, "Save my baby!" . . . and Papa Squirrel did the only sensible thing.

"Abandon ship!" he yelled as he and Mama Squirrel took a flying leap from the doomed tree. But Junior seemed to be frozen. The little squirrel squeezed his eyes shut, put both little paws over his ears, and waited for the crash.

I couldn't let that happen! With a spurt of raw energy, I caught the handles of the buggy with my front paws and hung on for dear life as I dug my back paws into the ground. Dirt sprayed up in all directions as my back paws dug a trench in the dirt the size of the Grand Canyon . . . deeper and deeper as the momentum of the buggy pulled me forward. But when the trench threatened to swallow me up to my nose—me, the fearless, noble mutt!—the baby buggy finally dragged to a stop . . . exactly three and a half inches from the big oak tree.

Silence.

I looked up. On the branch above my head, I saw Junior Squirrel dare to peek . . . and the little guy was so relieved to see that we hadn't crashed into the oak tree that he keeled over backwards in a dead faint.

Within seconds Matt the beagle and Rebecca the bassett hound caught up to me as I finally let go of the baby buggy and pulled myself out of the trench.

"Good job, Drea!" Matt and Rebecca cried, licking my face and sniffing me all over to make sure I was all right.

"Oh, thank heavens," cried the frightened mother, running up to the buggy and snatching up her giggling baby. After making sure the baby was all right, the mother turned to us as we lay sprawled on the grass . . . panting, exhausted and dirty. "What wonderful dogs!" she exclaimed. "You saved my baby!"

We sat up and wagged our tails wearily as the lady patted each one of us on the head. "I hope your master gives you all extra treats for dinner tonight," she gushed. "You certainly earned it."

As the mother placed her baby back in the buggy and started to push it away, the baby waved gleefully. "Doggies!" she gurgled.

"Did you hear that?" said the mother to her friend as they walked away. "Her first word!"

We three dogs watched proudly as the mother resumed her walk through the park—this time keeping a firm grip on the buggy handle.

"That sure was a cute baby," sighed Rebecca, squatting on her short, basset hound rump.

I nodded in agreement and flopped to the ground beside her. "I'm glad we were here to help out . . . but it didn't tell us much about Floyd."

But Matt the beagle was panting eagerly. "Yes, it did! I know where he is! . . . Let's go!"

Why Settle for Boring When You Can Give Floyd a Bath?

Well, E.D., as our Secret Adventure into dog land faded out of our imaginations, Matt leaped up from the grass and started to run.

"Hey! Where's he going?" I yelled. "C'mon, Rebecca—we can't lose him again!"

"Matt! Wait up!" Rebecca cried, running like crazy after her little brother as we followed him across the park and into the neighborhood on the other side.

"Where's he going?" I panted.

"I don't know!" Rebecca wailed.

Just then George's bike skidded to a stop two

feet in front of us. He looked terrible . . . which is hard to do, E.D., for a guy as good-looking as George.

"No sign of Matt downtown," he said, shaking his head grimly.

I pointed down the street, where Matt was just turning a corner. "We just found him!" I said. "But we're about to lose him again!"

"No prob," yelled George, jerking his bike around and taking off like a drag racer. "I'll catch him this time!"

And I swear, E.D., he took off so fast, it seemed like his bike left smoking tire tracks on the pavement!

We kept running, trying to keep up, turning where George turned . . . when suddenly the next street looked kinda familiar.

"This is the street you live on, Rebecca!" I gasped as we rounded the corner. But George had ridden past the Long's house and was waving to us from the driveway of a big colonial house several doors down.

"Over here!" he yelled, then disappeared around the side of the house.

We ran down the street and up the driveway. "Whose house is this?" I panted to Rebecca.

"The Carters . . . they're our neighbors," said Rebecca, gulping for air.

Just then George reappeared and beckoned to

us to come around to the back of the house. "You're not going to believe this," he said, grinning from ear to ear.

He got that right, E.D.

As we came around the corner of the house, there on the back patio was Matt . . . sitting on the ground and leaning against the Famous Missing Floyd, who didn't look at all sorry for running away and ruining a perfectly good Saturday morning. And Matt was holding the cutest little gray and white puppy on his lap, while a mommy sheepdog lay beside him nursing a whole litter of pint-size Floyds!

Matt grinned up at us. "I almost forgot . . . Floyd has responsibilities, too. He just became a dad!"

And believe it or not, E.D., Floyd was sitting there looking as proud as any papa I've ever seen, watching over his brood. Although . . . he did look a little silly with that stripe of green paint down his back.

We played with the puppies for a while . . . they are *so* cute. One in particular crawled all over me and tried to chew my finger. It's hard to imagine that Humongous Floyd was ever that tiny. I was so tempted to ask the Carters if I could have one of the puppies . . . and then I remembered my parents standing in the dining room doorway, dripping with paint and wallpaper, looking like something out of "The Aliens Have Landed!" and decided this wasn't the best weekend to bring up the subject of a puppy—especially one that looks like Floyd!

So now we're all back at my house, none the worse for wear . . . except it took a while to calm down my parents, who were borderline berserk when they came home from the hardware store to an empty house and didn't know where we were. That's because in all the excitement of losing Floyd and Matt, I forgot to leave them a note . . .

Matt and Rebecca were so pooped from the morning's adventure, that they both fell asleep reading books after lunch . . . which gave me this time, E.D., to catch up on things in my electronic diary.

But I guess I can't put off the inevitable any longer . . . I gotta give that rascal Floyd a B-A-T-H. Which—if last night's wild chase all over the house was a clue—I suspect he hates. And I also suspect I'm gonna regret not doing it last night, because that green stripe down his back has dried and hardened and may be just a *little* difficult to wash out . . . ya know, just a smidgen.

Whew. Is it only three o'clock on Saturday afternoon? It feels like three lifetimes since yesterday. Is this what parents feel like all the time? If so, I don't want to know!

Well, as my dad would say, E.D., hold the fort!—I'm off to hose down the livestock. And I sure hope I can make it through the next day and a half without any more disasters, adventures, missing persons, runaway animals, or green parents. Right now I'd even settle for *boring*.

Catch ya later, E.D. Over and out.

— *Click!* —

Well, E.D., I can say definitely that giving Floyd a bath is *not* boring.

I figured out this great plan for how to do it. First, I tied a rope to Floyd's collar so he couldn't get away. Then I enlisted Matt and Rebecca to hold onto his collar to help Floyd stand still. Then I wet him down with the hose . . . but he still managed to wiggle and jump around so much, that he kept knocking the kids over, and it seemed like more water got on Matt and Rebecca than on the dog.

But we finally got him hosed down, and he stood there trembling and whining like a big baby while Matt squirted some shampoo on him, and Rebecca and I took turns trying to scrub that green paint off his back. But that matted mess didn't budge for the longest time . . . I could almost hear the blobs of green paint chuckling to each other . . .

"Hey, Joe, you got a good grip on that dog hair?"

"You better believe it, Sam. Ain't had this much fun since this oversized pooch knocked the can of paint over last night and we splashed all over Drea's mom."

"How 'bout you, Butch?"

"Me, too . . . riding this here dog all over Hampton Falls sure beats decorating a wall. I ain't about to let go now."

"Hey, guys . . . don't this dog's fleas look good in green?"

"Heh, heh, heh! They're still mad as spit and as stuck as tar. Hey! Maybe we just discovered a new way to get rid of fleas . . . paint the dog!"

"Ha, ha! . . . oops, watch it, fellas! That Drea Thomas is aiming the water hose our way again!"

"Oh—oh—heh—heh—oh—ah—hahaha . . . that brush tickles!"

"Hang on, Butch! Hang on, Sam! Don't let her loosen your grip!"

Well, I wasn't going to let a few sassy paint blobs get the better of me. I finally used my wide-toothed comb to pry the individual dog hairs apart and comb out the paint. Believe me, E.D., I was learning the hard way not to put off a responsibility till later—it only gets harder. Not to mention paint and dog hair stuck in my comb. Yuuuck.

But we finally got most of the paint off Floyd's back, and I was rinsing him off with the hose, when I heard Grandpa Ben's voice calling from the driveway, "Hi, Drea . . . hi, kids. What's going on?"

I turned 'round to say hi . . . but I forgot I had the hose in my hand and . . . uh . . . well, let's put it this way, E.D.: Grandpa is now sitting in the kitchen wearing Dad's robe and slippers while his sopping wet clothes are tumbling in the clothes dryer.

Matt and Rebecca just stared in horror when I accidentally turned the hose on Grandpa . . . even Floyd seemed interested in this turn of events. I was so shocked, I didn't move for several seconds . . . until Grandpa began spluttering and waving me off. Then I dropped the hose and dived for the spigot to turn it off . . . and Matt and Rebecca were so surprised that they let go of Floyd . . . and Floyd thought this was a new game and went tearing around the yard on the end of the rope, and ended up rolling in the garden. By the time we dragged him out, he looked like a mud wrestler.

So then we had to give him a B-A-T-H all over again, and . . . I'm not going to bore you with the sordid details, E.D. But the D-O-G in question is lying here on my rug with his favorite toy pig in his paws, because my mother saw him shivering out in the backyard and felt sorry for him and said he could come up here until he completely dried off.

Oh . . . here comes Rebecca with her hair in a towel, so guess I'm next in line for a B-A-T-H. Then I gotta put all of our muddy clothes in the washing machine . . . sigh. Guess I'll have a full load this time.

Hey . . . I just realized there was so much insanity this morning that I totally forgot to ask George how the party went last night! Guess I'll call Kimberly later . . .

— *Click!* —

It's now ten p.m. and I'm under the covers wrapping up Day 4,861 in the Secret Adventures of Drea Thomas.

What's that new word we learned in English last week? Am-bu-lant . . . no . . . ambillient? . . . no . . . am-bi-va-lent—that's it. Ambivalent.

I'm feeling *ambivalent*, E.D.—which means feeling two conflicting ways about the same thing. I mean, I should be happy that the audio scavenger hunt was an absolute blast, with everyone telling Cristan that it was the best birthday party ever—right? But to be honest, E.D., I wish the whole thing had been totally boring so I wouldn't feel so bad about missing the party.

Kimberly said George did a great job organizing

the scavenger hunt in my place . . . oh, get this, E.D. Kimberly said she almost told Cristan and her mother that I couldn't come to the party because I'd just come down with Rocky Mountain Spotted Fever . . . but then she realized I'd either have to stay out of school at least six weeks or die to pull it off, so instead she just told them in a mysterious voice that I was "unavoidably detained."

Anyway . . . George divided up everybody into four teams—he only brought four Walkmans, I guess. George led one team, Bobby another, and Kimberly and Cristan the other two, with both guys and girls on each team. He gave each group the list I'd created of people they had to find and interview . . . let's see, I think the list included a police officer or security guard, taxi driver, store clerk, someone under ten, a college student, a senior citizen, someone delivering pizza, a couple walking hand-in-hand, and . . . and . . . oh, yeah, a dog-walker. And they were supposed to ask each person what was the craziest thing he or she ever did, and the funniest thing that ever happened to them.

Bobby's team won with the most people interviewed . . . his team was the only one that found someone delivering pizza—to a security guard at the mall, no less! And Kimberly said *everyone* must have interviewed the same college student, because when her team asked this young guy playing a sax what was the craziest thing that ever happened to him, he threw up his hands and said, "Deciding to play my sax near a mall on a Friday night! Here I am, just minding my own business, trying to make a little change so I can get home to Chicago for Thanksgiving . . . and at least a hundred kids have interrupted my Sonny Rollins tune asking me stupid questions. Now, are you guys gonna put some money in my case or not?"

Hmm . . . I wonder if my dad the music professor knows his college sax players are moonlighting at the mall?

Anyway . . . Kimberly's going to bring me all four cassette tapes tomorrow. Everybody at the party listened to each other's tapes after the scavenger hunt while they slurped down pizza and cherry cheesecake . . . she says they're a scream.

Oh, yeah. Kimberly said Cristan liked my stuffed penguin. I *am* glad about that. It sure beats a certain rubber pig I'm baby-sitting this weekend. If I step on it and it *squeals* at me one more time, I'll . . . never mind.

Mom and Dad are still slopping paint in the dining room—making up for lost time, I guess. But Matt and Rebecca are asleep in their sleeping bags on my floor. Yawwwnnn . . . guess I'll turn in, too. Only one more day to go in the Longest Weekend of Drea Thomas's life.

Catch ya tomorrow, E.D.

— *Click!* —

Déjà Vu and Catastrophe, Too

Drea Thomas checking in, E.D.

Day 4,862, Sunday afternoon . . . time: fifteen hundred hours . . . and all's quiet on the Thomas front today, thank goodness. When we got home from church, Mom and Dad asked me to make lunch for the kids so they could try to get the dining room paint-and-wallpaper job finished today. Matt and Rebecca voted for tomato soup and toasted cheese sandwiches . . . but you know me, E.D., I can't make just *plain* toasted cheese sandwiches. So while Rebecca dumped two cans of tomato soup into a pot, Matt and I invented a Thomas-Long Special: bread, ranch dressing, cheddar cheese, salami, more cheese, more dressing, and another slice of bread. Then we buttered—or maybe I should say, "margarined"—the outsides of the bread and grilled 'em on the electric griddle.

'Course, my imaginary friend the toaster just couldn't keep his mouth shut, since (I tell the kids) he thinks he owns the kitchen, and we only cook and eat there with his permission . . .

"Well, well, look who's taking over the kitchen," sniffed Mr. Toaster, wiggling his handles. "Some pal you are, Drea Thomas . . . making TOAST-ed cheese sandwiches without even a polite nod to your loyal and hard-working TOAST-er. Instead, you give my job to

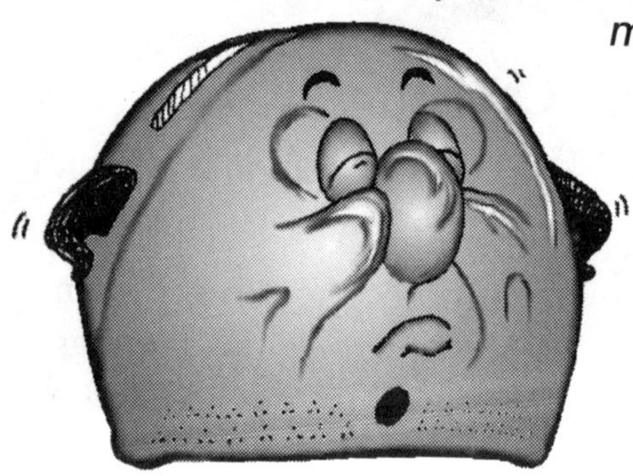

some new-fangled, modern thingumajig like that . . . that . . . flat electric gizmo there. Humph. So that's all the thanks I get for toasting toast for the Thomas toast-eaters for forty years . . ."

I leaned both elbows on the counter and eyeballed the toaster. "Are you through complaining?" I asked mildly.

"Complaining? Who's complaining?" pro-

tested the toaster. "I'm just speaking my mind . . . tellin' it like it is . . . stating my opinion . . . after all, it's a free country, isn't it?"

"Well, yes, it is," I agreed. "And if you'd like, I'll stuff one of these toasted cheese sandwiches in your slots . . . but I'm warning ya, Toaster ol' buddy. It takes a looong time to get melted cheese off your wires. Might even cause a short in your circuits. Then where would you be? Up in a box in the attic, waiting for the flea market sale next Memorial Day . . ."

"Whoa, Nellie!" huffed the toaster. "Let's not be hasty here. I was just making conversation . . ."

"Yeah, right," I grinned. "And I was just making toasted cheese sandwiches."

Matt laughed at my little dialogue with Mr. Toaster. "Hey, Drea," he suggested, "why *don't* we try toasting the cheese sandwiches in the toaster?"

"No way, José!" I said hastily. "I learned my lesson when I was three years old and tried to 'toast' little plastic records."

I'm not sure why Matt thought that was so funny, but he laughed so hard he fell off his chair.

Rebecca rolled her eyes—she has eye-rolling down to a fine art—and served up the soup like the Frugal Gourmet.

We made some extra sandwiches for Mom and Dad, and they took exactly four and a half minutes to eat before they disappeared back into the dining room, muttering something about not wanting their brushes to dry out.

Now Matt's out in the backyard playing with Floyd—under threat of dire consequences if he so much as sets a toenail outside the yard!—and Rebecca's doing her homework. I just finished—

Oops. There's the phone.

— Click! —

Back again. That was Grandpa on the phone, E.D., asking if I would help him pick the last of the tomatoes later this afternoon. I said okay . . . after Mrs. Long picks up the kids.

Guess I should have Matt and Rebecca pack their stuff, so that they're ready when she arrives. I'm feeling pretty good that we've gone a whole twenty-four hours and haven't had to declare a national emergency—

Oh, there's the back doorbell. Maybe that's Mrs. Long now.

Over and out, E.D.

— Click! —

I'm back and . . . wait a sec. What did I say just before signing off? Something about how good I was feeling. Here . . . let me rewind this thing a little way . . .

— Click! —

I can't believe it! My exact words before signing off were: "I'm feeling pretty good that we've gone a whole twenty-four hours and haven't had to declare a national emergency" . . . and then the doorbell rang.

But it wasn't Mrs. Long, E.D. It was Kimberly . . . she came over to bring me the audiotapes from Cristan's birthday party scavenger hunt and to model the new outfit she bought at Flashions Once-a-Year Sale yesterday. We listened to a couple of the tapes . . . some of the answers were an absolute scream.

Get this: a taxi driver said the craziest thing he ever did was let his brother-in-law talk him into going *bungee jumping*. His sweatpants caught on the tower when he jumped and were pulled right off. There he was, bouncing up and down in the air in his shorts!

Then there was the store clerk who said the craziest thing she ever did was try to "ride" inside a big oversized clothes dryer in a laundromat when she was a kid! But she *also* said that she got so dizzy she threw up afterwards . . . and got in BIG trouble with the manager who caught her!

Boy, E.D. . . . and some people think kids *today* act crazy!

Oh, yeah . . . some little kid said the craziest thing he ever did was stick a marble up his nose on a dare—and he had to go to the emergency room to have it taken out! Personally, E.D., I don't think that was crazy . . . it was stupid! A *marble* up his nose????

Anyway . . . enough about the scavenger hunt tapes.

Then Kimberly modeled her new outfit which is . . . uh, rather hard to describe. It was a fancy dress . . . a bright red skirt with a kinda short, flared overskirt, and the top was a big-collar top over a shell thing . . . Anyway. It was the kind of outfit that if *I* wore it, I'd look like the "Duracell Bunny Goes Hollywood." But I had to admit that Kimberly looked . . . well, stunning.

"It's very . . . retro," I told her. "In a progressive kind of way. Very you."

She was pleased. "Thank you," she said. But as she got ready to leave, she laid it on thick. "You really should have been there, Drea. There were some great vests on sale, too."

I shrugged. "I did the right thing by staying," I told her. And I meant it, too. In spite of the Dining Room Disaster Friday night, and the Hunt for the Truant Dog Saturday morning . . . oh, yes, and the

Bath Fiasco Saturday afternoon . . . it's been kinda fun having Matt and Rebecca around all weekend, and it makes me feel good that Mrs. Long trusts me enough to ask me to take care of them.

Kimberly sighed. "I know . . . responsibility and all that," she admitted. "Just don't pass it around."

She opened the back door to leave . . . and who should be standing there, but Mrs. Long, her hand raised to knock on the door, and if she hadn't stopped, she would have knocked on Kimberly's face.

"Hello again, Kimberly," said Mrs. Long as she came into the kitchen, in a weren't-you-here-when-I-dropped-the-kids-off? tone of voice.

Kimberly blinked in astonishment. "Déjà vu or what?" she whispered to me.

I called for the kids, who appeared with their backpacks. After they'd hugged their mom, Matt ran outside to untie Floyd. At the moment I didn't notice, because Mrs. Long handed me a package. "I saw this in the boutique at the hotel," she said, smiling. "I thought it would look perfect on you. So, here's a little extra thank-you for giving up your weekend to help me."

I opened the package and pulled out a beautiful vest—just the kind I wanted, with a black, silky back and kind of a tapestry print on the front.

"I can't believe it!" I gasped. I had totally missed the Flashions Once-a-Year Sale . . . and ended up with the greatest vest ever, anyway!

I could tell Kimberly was impressed, too. "Great vest," she agreed.

"We gotta pack up Floyd's things," Rebecca reminded me, picking up his bowls and toys and stuffing them into Floyd's backpack.

I picked up the silly pink rubber pig. "See ya, Squeaky," I murmured . . .

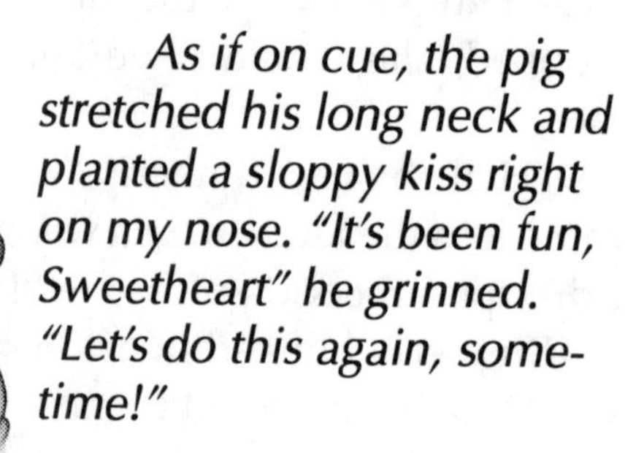

As if on cue, the pig stretched his long neck and planted a sloppy kiss right on my nose. "It's been fun, Sweetheart" he grinned. "Let's do this again, sometime!"

I rubbed my nose and looked around to see if anyone else was watching . . . but I guess it was just my imagination. So I stuffed the pig in with the rest of Floyd's things.

Meanwhile, Mrs. Long was making conversation with Kimberly. "So, what's new in your life?" she asked pleasantly.

Kimberly looked blank. "Hmmm . . . oh, I know! My parents might take me to England this summer. My dad has to go on business, so he's taking the whole family . . . but I can't remember the name of the exact place," Kimberly said.

Mrs. Long tried to be helpful. "London? . . . Stratford-on-Avon? . . ."

Kimberly shook her head. "No . . . it has something to do with some health springs discoverd by the Romans ages ago . . . oh, I know! *Bath*!"

At the word "Bath," Floyd, standing in the open doorway with Matt, suddenly perked up his ears . . .

"Ohhhh, NOOOOOOOO!" Rebecca screamed.

"Ohhhh, NOOOOOOOO!" Matt screamed.

"Ohhhh, NOOOOOOOO!" I screamed.

Floyd jerked away in a SNAP, scrambling in dog panic around the slippery kitchen floor . . . and then made a beeline for the swinging dining room door.

It was like a slow-motion movie, E.D. I saw Floyd's tail disappear through those doors . . . heard a bump . . . then a screech . . . then a crash!

No one moved in the kitchen. We just stood there like petrified statues. When the dining room door finally opened . . . there stood Mom and Dad like a rerun of a B-movie on late-night TV: Dad once again plastered with a strip of wallpaper, and Mom's head and shoulders covered—and I mean *covered*—in green paint.

No one spoke for the longest time, E.D. . . . at least a million years, I'm sure. Even Floyd knew something was wrong and crouched on the floor, looking guilty.

"Then again," Kimberly said timidly, "maybe it was somewhere in France . . ."

Picking Up the Pieces

As I see it, E.D., at that moment my parents had two options: either have a screaming fit then and there . . . or break down and cry. So I was shocked when they began to laugh hysterically instead. First a strangled giggle from my mom, then a snort and snicker from my dad, and finally full-scale belly laughs, with both of them leaning against the dining room doorway in helpless hysteria.

So then Matt and Rebecca started to giggle, and even Mrs. Long laughed nervously. Only Kimberly and I stood openmouthed, staring at everybody as if they were crazy.

This was the state Grandpa found us in when he showed up at the back door. He slowly looked from my parents, clad in wallpaper and green paint . . . to the cowering dog . . . to Matt and Rebecca . . . and finally to me. Then he said mildly, "Looks like I've missed all the fun."

Well, that did it. We *all* laughed hysterically then.

When all the laughter finally died down, Mrs. Long wanted to help clean up the mess in the dining room, but Mom and Dad encouraged her to take the kids—and Floyd!—home after her long trip. Frankly, E.D., I suspect their motives weren't exactly noble.

Kimberly tried to sneak out in the general exodus, but I grabbed her, steered her upstairs to my room, made her take off her fancy dress, put on some of my old grubbies, and join the cleanup crew in the dining room. Luckily the drop cloths had caught most of the spilled paint—other than drenching my mom, that is—so all we had to do was wash off the paint splatters from the baseboards, the door, and other places like that. Grandpa helped, too, and we had most of it done by the time my mom got out of the longest shower in history, looking like a pink, wrinkled prune after trying to wash all the green paint out of her hair and ears and eyelashes.

I finally let Kimberly go . . . but only after I looked up in our world atlas and found out that there really *is* a town called Bath in England. (There is.) Otherwise, I was going to accuse her of teasing

Floyd with the word *bath* on purpose!

Now that everyone's gone, I feel this huge wave of relief washing over me . . . uh, on second thought, I need another metaphor. I can't think of "water" without thinking of the B-WORD!

Anyway . . . all my weekend responsibilities are finally over. Well, almost. I still have to pick tomatoes with Grandpa. Oh . . . I see him out there in the garden. Groan. Guess I better stop talking to you, E.D., and give him a hand like I promised.

Over and out.

— *Click!* —

Back again, E.D., and now Grandpa's gone, too. But after all the commotion this afternoon, it was actually kinda peaceful going out to the garden.

The two of us just stood there for a few minutes, looking at the garden. It really looked good after all the weeding and snail catching we did last week. The late tomatoes hung heavy on their vines, looking fat and ripe and juicy. But this time I knew they didn't get that way in a SNAP, and there was a lot of hard work and responsibility that went into it.

"How does it look to you, Drea?" Grandpa asked me.

"It all looks so beautiful, I almost hate to pick them," I admitted. I liked the way the garden looked at that moment, and kinda wished it would stay that way all fall and winter. But . . . that was silly. If we didn't pick them, they'd rot on the vines, and all our work would be for nothing. "But I guess picking them is part of being responsible for the garden, too, huh?" I added.

Grandpa grinned from ear to ear. "I think you're going to make a very good gardener," he said, and gave me a big hug. And somehow Grandpa's approval was all the reward I needed for tackling some pretty big—make that hairy!—responsibilities this past week.

"Now's the fun part," Grandpa said gleefully, and starting picking the tomatoes and putting them in his basket.

I tugged at a lush tomato, and it practically fell into my hand . . . and it felt so plump and juicy and good that I couldn't help myself. I sank my teeth into the sweet, juicy fruit . . . and the next thing I knew, tomato juice was squirting in at least five directions! All down my shirt . . . right into Grandpa's face . . .

I stared, aghast, as Grandpa slowly pulled out his handkerchief and wiped off his tomato-spattered glasses. Then he eyed the juice dripping off my chin which was making a little red river down my shirt. "Looks like you'll be doing an extra load of *lawn*-dry today, Drea," he said dryly.

Ah-ha! I thought. *The bad puns are making a comeback.*

"Who, me, Grandpa?" I said, deliberately taking another bite of the tomato and sending another squirt in his direction. "Don't you think *weed* better do it together? We're a team, remember?"

"Sorry, Drea," Grandpa said, trying to keep a straight face as he mopped the latest squirt off his forehead. "This time the responsibility is in your *corn*-er."

"Well . . . then," I said, stuffing the rest of the tomato in my mouth and trying to spit tomato seeds at him, "you better keep up your *gard-en* your old age!"

Grandpa looked puzzled. "Keep up my . . .?" Then he burst out laughing. "Ohh, ho ho. Keep up my *guard in* my old age . . . ha, ha, ha! You got me that time, Drea!"

Somehow, between bad puns, tomato seeds, and laughing ourselves sick, we still managed to pick fifteen pounds of the best-tasting tomatoes this side of the Atlantic!

Well, anyway, E.D. . . . it's the end of Day 4,862 in the Secret Adventures of Drea Thomas and time to sign off my electronic diary . . . and that *is* something I can do in a SNAP!

— *Click!* —